McTAVISH
ON THE MOVE

McTAVISH
ON THE MOVE

Meg Rosoff

CANDLEWICK PRESS

Text copyright © 2019 by Meg Rosoff
Original illustrational style and cover art copyright © 2019 by Grace Easton
Interior illustrations by copy artist David Shephard,
based on and in the style of Grace Easton

First US edition 2022
First published by Barrington Stoke Ltd. (Great Britain) 2019

Library of Congress Catalog Card Number 2021947460
ISBN 978-1-5362-1376-8

22 23 24 25 26 27 LBM 10 9 8 7 6 5 4 3 2 1

Printed in Melrose Park, IL, USA

This book was typeset in Lora.

Candlewick Press
99 Dover Street
Somerville, Massachusetts 02144

www.candlewick.com

A JUNIOR LIBRARY GUILD SELECTION

CONTENTS

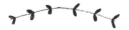

1

A Nice Day at Work

At six p.m. precisely, Pa Peachey stepped in through the front door singing a happy little tune.

"La, la, la," he sang. "Tra-la, tra-lee, oh happy me!"

Ollie and Ava sat at the kitchen table doing homework. They glanced at each other in alarm.

The Peachey family was used to Pa

Peachey returning from work cranky and crabby and crotchety. They were used to him mumbling and grumbling and muttering. But singing and smiling? Humming a happy tune?

"*La-di-da, la-di-dee, oh what joy it is to be!*" Pa Peachey sang.

Betty stared at her father with concern.

"Are you feeling quite well, Pa?" she asked.

"Quite well?" Pa Peachey answered. "Why, I am more than quite well! I am full of the joys of spring!"

Ava's eyes widened with horror.

Pa Peachey began to sing once more. "*If you're happy and you know it, clap your hands,*" he sang happily.

Nobody clapped. Ava and Ollie clutched each other in fear.

On his bed under the stairs, McTavish tilted his head, amazed. Never since McTavish joined the Peachey family had Pa Peachey come home from work in a good mood.

"Hello, darling," Ma Peachey said cautiously. "Are you feeling quite well?"

"Quite well? Quite well? Why does everyone keep asking if I'm feeling quite well? As a matter of fact, I am feeling superb. I am feeling devil-may-care and happy-go-lucky. I'm feeling joyous, optimistic, and downright delighted. Why, I am in such high spirits, I might dance a merry little dance!"

Ava covered her face with her hands.

"Perhaps you should sit down, Pa," Betty said, her brow furrowed.

"Perhaps we should call a doctor," Ollie said. "Or the police."

McTavish stood up. He padded across the room and sat at Pa Peachey's feet. He looked up at Pa Peachey's face.

Pa Peachey certainly looked like the same person who had left for work this morning in his usual grumpy mood. But perhaps he had been hit by a bus. Perhaps a blow to the head had changed his personality or given him amnesia. Perhaps Pa Peachey had forgotten his reputation as the world's crankiest man.

"Did you have a nice day at work?" Ma Peachey asked in a worried voice.

"As a matter of fact, I did," said Pa Peachey, smiling broadly.

The Peachey children froze. They stared at one another in disbelief.

"You had a nice day at work?" Ollie gaped. "Are you sure?"

"Really?" said Ava. "You had a *nice day*"— she pronounced the words carefully—"*at work?*"

"Indeed I did," Pa Peachey said with a huge grin.

The Peachey children shuddered.

McTavish pricked his ears, alert to this strange turn of events.

For a long time, nobody said a word. The silence was so silent, you could hear a pin stand still.

After a few minutes, Pa Peachey became impatient.

"Doesn't anyone want to know *why* I had a nice day at work?"

The Peachey children did not want to know.

Pa Peachey had never had a nice day at work. Not ever. Pa Peachey hated work almost as much as he hated weekends and holidays. He was crabby on Mondays and irritable on Tuesdays. On Wednesdays he was glum. On Thursdays and Fridays he was just plain cranky. Pa Peachey complained about beautiful summer days. He moaned about Christmas. He hated weddings and birthdays. In short, Pa Peachey was not known for his cheerful disposition.

The Peachey children did not mind Pa Peachey's personality. They were used to it.

What they did not like was unexpected change.

"If you are going to be happy all of a sudden," said Ollie, "I wish you would give us time to prepare."

"If you are planning to be jolly," Ava said, "I'd appreciate at least a week's notice."

"Are you running a fever, Pa?" Betty asked with concern.

"What has it come to," moaned Pa Peachey, "when a man with a new job isn't allowed to be cheerful in his own home?"

"A new job!" exclaimed Betty.

"Tell us," said Ma Peachey.

"Well," said Pa Peachey, "if you must know—"

"We must!" shouted all the Peacheys at once.

"I have been offered a new job."

"A new job!" Betty leaped up and hugged her father. "That is wonderful news!"

Ma Peachey frowned. "What sort of new job?"

The Peacheys fell silent once more. They tilted their heads. They squinted their eyes. They concentrated hard.

The fact was that not one of them understood what Pa Peachey did at work, despite his many attempts over the years to explain.

"It has to do with . . ." Pa Peachey began.

The Peacheys leaned in, attentive.

Pa Peachey looked at the ceiling. "It's rather like . . ."

The Peacheys all frowned with concentration.

Pa Peachey looked down at the floor. "It's very much concerned with . . ."

Nobody even dared blink.

Pa Peachey closed his eyes for a long moment. At last he opened them and sighed.

"Never mind," he said. "The new job is rather like the old job—only more so."

All the Peacheys nodded wisely.

Pa Peachey hesitated for a moment and then went on. "Perhaps I should also mention—not that it is at all important, influential, or significant in any way, not that any of you will even be terribly interested—"

"Yes?" Betty said with a slight narrowing of the eyes.

"That the new job will be . . ."

"Yes?" Ava said with the beginnings of a frown.

"The new job will be?" said Ollie with a suspicious glare.

"The new job will be," Pa Peachey said, "in a different place."

"A different place?" Ollie gasped. "What does that even mean? Paris? Albania? Idaho? Shanghai?"

Ava frowned. "When you say 'a different place,' what sort of different place do you have in mind?"

Betty looked puzzled. "Does 'a different place' mean 'a place' that is 'different'?"

McTavish listened carefully. As a rescue dog, he knew it was his sworn duty to rescue the Peachey family from danger and harm. He had rescued them many times in the past. The challenge, he found, was to *keep* them rescued, for the Peacheys had a bad habit of descending into chaos the moment he turned his back.

McTavish did not remember turning his back lately, but he nonetheless had a feeling that chaos might be lurking just around the corner.

2

A NEW JOB

Ma Peachey wanted to speak to Pa Peachey alone. So Ollie, Ava, and Betty trudged upstairs. They lay on Ava's bed, their faces grim.

"What do you suppose he means by 'a different place'?" asked Betty.

"I suspect he means 'a different place,'" said Ava. "A new job in a place that is different from this place."

"Hang on," Ollie said, eyes wide. "You don't mean a new house, do you? I don't want a new house."

"I love this house," Betty cried. "I've lived here since I was born. In fact, I've lived here since before I was born."

"'To live is to suffer," Ava said, shaking her head and quoting from one of her favorite German philosophers.

Betty and Ollie looked at Ava. They were silent for some time.

"What if it's a better job?" Betty asked at last. "What if it's a job that will make Pa Peachey cheerful all the time?"

"Don't be ridiculous," said Ava.

"No such job exists," said Ollie.

They lay in silence, thinking gloomy thoughts, until Ma Peachey called them downstairs once more.

"Could someone please tell us what is happening?" Ollie asked.

"What will be the fate of our poor doomed family?" Betty asked.

"Must we leave our happy home and leap blindly into the dark unknown?" Ava asked.

Ma Peachey began putting plates on the table for dinner. "What is happening is that Pa Peachey has been offered an excellent new job. He would like to take it. I would like him to take it. There is only one small problem."

"Only one?" said Ollie.

"A problem?" said Ava.

"How small?" said Betty.

"If Pa Peachey takes the job, we will have to move house."

"I knew it!" said Ava.

"No way," said Ollie.

"That is not a small problem," said Betty.

3

NOT A SMALL PROBLEM

"I'm not going," said Ollie.

"Neither am I," said Ava.

Betty got down from the table and sat with McTavish on the floor. She hugged him tight. "Don't worry, McTavish. Ma Peachey was not serious when she said we must leave our happy home. She was making a joke."

"No, she wasn't," said Ollie.

"No, I wasn't," said Ma Peachey. "But we

will find a new house that every one of us likes just as much as the old house. Maybe even more."

"Never," said Ollie.

"Impossible," said Ava.

"It is not impossible," said Ma Peachey in her most stern voice. But when she saw a tear roll down Betty's cheek, she bent down and hugged her. "Don't worry, Betty. It will all turn out fine. Change can be exciting and fun. Sometimes even more fun than staying the same."

"We won't have to change anything else, will we?" Ollie asked with a suspicious glare.

"Well," said Ma Peachey, "Ollie, you will be changing schools next year anyway. Ava can stay at her old school."

Everybody looked at Betty.

"Unfortunately, Betty will have to change schools."

"I don't want to change schools," Betty cried. "I like my school. I know which teachers are terrible and which teachers are nice. I know which boys are friendly and which are spiteful. I know which desks have gum stuck underneath. I know never to eat Miss Biffo's meatball surprise on Tuesday or her mystery upside-down cake on Friday. It has taken many years of careful study to get the hang of my school."

The tears in Betty's eyes crawled down her cheeks. McTavish put his head in her lap.

McTavish was an extremely sympathetic dog. Besides, he did not want to move any more than Betty did. He liked his park. He liked his dog friends. He knew that Lexi

and Nico were friendly dogs. He knew that George liked to play chase. He knew that Toffee ran too fast and Treacle ran too slow. He knew how to swim in the pond when the park ranger wasn't looking and where small children sometimes dropped delicious things to eat.

But McTavish was also a practical dog.

I shall have to be very clever about this moving business, he thought. *Pa Peachey is unnaturally happy, Betty is unnaturally sad, and the usual order of the Peachey family has been thrown into a terrible state of chaos.*

McTavish sighed. It took a particularly clever dog to sniff out solutions to all the chaos this family created.

"I think," Pa Peachey said, "that we shall talk about the subject of moving . . . later."

The Peachey children slumped.

They knew what *We'll talk about this later* meant. It meant *We will not talk about this ever again because it has all been decided.* It meant *We are the grown-ups and we make all the decisions.* It meant *You are the children and have to do as we say.* It meant *If you don't like it, too bad.*

The Peachey children couldn't wait to grow up so they could destroy the lives of their own innocent children.

McTavish went back to his bed under the stairs and began to think.

4

DOOM AND GLOOM

A general feeling of dejection fell upon the Peachey family, except of course for Pa Peachey, who hummed and whistled cheerfully day and night and said things like "What a lovely day!" and "Smile! It might never happen!"

The Peachey children found this last expression particularly annoying, as *it* looked almost certain to happen.

Ava resigned herself to a life of suffering and unhappiness, which her books on German philosophy said was the natural state of humankind.

Ollie kept hoping a miracle might happen that would change his parents' minds about moving.

Betty just wanted the whole subject of moving to go away and hoped it might disappear if she never thought about it again.

But Pa Peachey continued to whistle and act cheerful, which filled his children with a terrible gloom.

The weekend arrived.

Pa Peachey buttered his toast and sang a happy song over breakfast.

"*Oh how merry, oh what glee! I am as happy as a tree,*" he sang.

"Happy as a tree?" Ollie muttered. "How happy is that? Why not happy as a pebble? Or a hammer? Or an armadillo?"

Betty and Ava glowered at their father.

"Well," Ma Peachey said, "Pa Peachey and I think we may have found a new house to buy. I think we should all go and have a look."

"No," said Betty, folding her arms firmly over her chest.

"Definitely not," Ollie said.

"*Quelle horreur*," Ava muttered. *Quelle horreur* is what French philosophers always say when they think about the meaning of life.

Ma Peachey put her hands on her hips. "Now, now. You never know. You might like the new house even more than the one we have now."

"Impossible," said Betty, sniffing loudly

and wiping her nose on her sleeve.

Pa Peachey was in high spirits. "One door closes, another door opens," he said with a happy smile.

"One door closes, another door slams," grumbled Ollie.

"There are no problems, only opportunities," Pa Peachey said with a cheerful chuckle.

"According to Nietzsche, that which does not kill us makes us stronger," Ava said. "I sincerely hope that this moving malarkey does not kill us."

Pa Peachey began to dance a happy little jig, which caused Ollie to grind his teeth and Ava to make a noise like a screeching cat.

Betty burst into tears.

"That's the spirit," Pa Peachey said cheerfully.

*

Once Betty had stopped crying and Ollie had stopped glowering, they all piled into the family car and set off for the new neighborhood.

McTavish stuck his head out the window. He let his ears fly behind him and kept a beady eye on the route.

Ava scrunched up in the corner of the back seat reading a book about suffering by the Austrian philosopher Wittgenstein.

Ollie stared unhappily ahead, imagining the new neighborhood as a dismal landscape, barren like the moon, or the sort of place in which a fire has destroyed all signs of life.

Betty hugged McTavish.

At last Ma Peachey stopped the car.

Pa Peachey turned to the children. "Ta-da!" he said.

The Peacheys stepped out of the car. They saw trees and houses. They saw grass and birds. They saw children playing games. They saw squirrels chattering in trees.

They saw a house with a FOR SALE sign in front of it.

The house was mainly white. It had a blue front door. An apple tree grew in the yard. Tulips nodded by the path. The house looked friendly. McTavish jumped out of the car and ran straight up the path. He peed on the apple tree.

"So," said Pa Peachey, "what do you think of our new house?

5

THE NEW HOUSE

Ollie couldn't help noticing that the new neighborhood didn't look very different from the old neighborhood. He saw no blasted heath. He saw no piles of rubble or rolls of barbed wire. The grass looked green and the people looked friendly.

Ava noticed that the new house looked a teensy bit like the old house.

Except for the apple tree in the front yard.

And the fact that her bedroom had its own bathroom, one she didn't have to share with Ollie and Betty.

The new house had a laundry chute that went from the second floor all the way down to the laundry room in the cellar.

Ollie had found the top of the laundry chute and was peering into it, wondering whether he could jump in and slide down, when Ma Peachey's face appeared at the bottom of the chute.

"Don't even think about it," she said.

"Maybe the new house is not so bad after all," Ollie said, saving the chute for another day.

"Maybe I could just about manage to live here," said Ava, thinking about how nice it would be to have a bath with nobody pounding on the door asking how long she would be.

McTavish looked at Betty. "Woof!" he said, and ran into the closet in Betty's bedroom.

"McTavish?" she called. But there was no sign of him.

Betty crouched down and crawled to the back of her closet, where she found a small, half-open door.

"McTavish?" she called again.

"Woof!" came the answer from within.

Betty squeezed through the door after McTavish and found herself in a tiny hidden room with an even tinier round window overlooking the yard.

What a perfect private clubhouse, Betty thought. She could sit here all day and nobody would know where she was or what she was doing. What a perfect secret place to read and think and hide and make plans.

For the first time all day, she forgot to frown.

After a while, Betty and McTavish crawled out of the little room. Together they explored and sniffed every corner of the new bedroom. There were lots of shelves for Betty's books and two big windows overlooking some trees. The room was sunny. It was painted a very boring shade of blue, but Betty thought she might repaint it a bright shade of yellow.

If she agreed to move, that is.

Betty and McTavish explored the rest of the house. Then they explored the front, side, and back yards. There was a wall at the bottom of the backyard with a gate that led directly into a large public park. The park was full of people and dogs. It looked like the perfect sort of park for a dog like McTavish.

"I think McTavish might need a walk," Ma Peachey said. "Betty, why don't you and Ollie take him to the park?"

Betty fetched McTavish's leash, and off they went. They ran on ahead while Ollie lagged behind, staring at his phone in what he hoped was the cool sort of way that made girls want to be your girlfriend.

They'd only walked a short distance when a whippet raced up to McTavish and began running circles around him.

When at last the whippet stopped, she had a conversation with McTavish that went like this:

"Woooo," said the whippet.

"Ufff," said McTavish.

"Aroou-ooo," said the whippet.

"Urrruff!" said McTavish.

Having discovered that they had much in common, the two dogs ran off together. McTavish and the whippet chased each other from one tree to the next and back again. It was an excellent game. The whippet was very fast, but McTavish was clever and cut corners to keep up. When at last they came to a halt, panting and happy, a girl ran up carrying a leash.

"There you are, Jess, you bad dog!" she said. "Didn't you hear me calling?"

"She's not really a bad dog," Betty said. "I think she's just excited to meet McTavish."

"McTavish is very cute," said the girl, who looked about Betty's age. "What breed is he?"

"Well," said Betty, "he is part Scottish

terrier, part Bichon Frisé, part poodle, part Jack Russell—and part Tibetan spaniel."

"Goodness," said the girl. "I'm Jasmin, by the way. My dog is Jess. And that," she said, pointing to a very cool-looking person staring at her phone nearby, "is my older sister Jade."

"Nice to meet you, Jasmin. My name is Betty."

Ollie, who had been pretending to not know Betty and McTavish, suddenly appeared at their side.

"I'm Ollie," said Ollie to Jasmin. "Is that your sister over there?"

Jasmin giggled. "Yes, that's my sister."

"She looks very cool," said Ollie. "By the way, this is my dog, McTavish."

"Your dog?" said Jasmin.

"Your dog?" said Betty.

Your dog? thought McTavish.

Ollie ignored them. "Do you live nearby?"

Jasmin nodded.

"Great! Our dogs can be friends," Ollie said, wondering if Jade might agree to be his girlfriend.

Jess ran off after a squirrel.

"Bye for now," shouted Jasmin, running after Jess.

"Bye, Jess! Bye, Jasmin!" Betty waved.

"Bye, Jade," Ollie called to Jade, who ignored him. "See you around!"

Ollie and Betty walked together for a few minutes, and then Ollie said, "Maybe I should be the one holding McTavish."

But Betty gripped the leash tight. "McTavish is my dog," she said. "Not some kind of furry bait for catching girlfriends."

She glared at Ollie, but it was no good.

She knew exactly what he was thinking. Once they moved, he would take McTavish to the park as often as possible. As a kind of furry bait for catching girlfriends.

They circled back to the car.

"So?" Pa Peachey asked, chuckling happily. "What do you think of the new house?"

"OK by me," Ava said with a shrug.

"Fine," said Ollie.

They all looked for Betty, but she was already sitting in the car with McTavish, windows and doors shut, waiting to go home.

6

GETTING READY TO MOVE

Ollie was excited about moving because Jade lived nearby and might agree to be his girlfriend. Once they met.

Ava didn't mind moving because she would no longer have to share a bathroom with Ollie or Betty.

Ma Peachey didn't mind moving (except for all the packing and unpacking) because the new house had a nice sunny office for her on the top floor, and also because she wanted Pa Peachey to be happy with his new job.

McTavish didn't mind moving because he liked the new park and he liked his new friend Jess.

Pa Peachey continued to stroll around whistling like a demented canary, which made everyone edgy.

But as the date for moving approached, Betty minded more and more.

She liked her old house.

She liked her old school.

She didn't want to be the new girl.

She didn't want to make new friends.

What if no one at the new school liked her?

What if her new teachers were horrible?

What if her classmates knew more than she did about everything?

What if she got lost on the first day?

What if nobody helped her?

What if nobody wanted to talk to her ever again?

Meanwhile, the rest of the Peacheys packed, made lists, and sorted through drawers. They cleared shelves, threw things away, and put labels on boxes. They were so busy that nobody really noticed Betty.

Even Ma Peachey forgot to notice Betty.

But McTavish noticed, because McTavish was a very noticing sort of dog. In particular, he noticed everything that happened to Betty. When Betty was happy, McTavish was happy. When Betty was sad, McTavish was sad.

At the moment, Betty was sad.

McTavish lay on his bed with his head on his front paws and considered the facts.

He had moved many times. He had left his littermates and moved to his first home on his own. He had moved from his first home to the shelter when his owner became too old to look after him. He had moved from the shelter to the Peacheys' home. And now he was moving to another house with the Peacheys.

Throughout all these moves, McTavish had noticed that the best way to make new friends was to be friendly and optimistic.

Betty was convinced her new life would be a disaster, but McTavish had a feeling she might be wrong.

He thought very hard about how to convince Betty to be optimistic.

Thinking is very tiring, even for a dog as clever as McTavish.

Which is why, after a short time, he fell asleep.

7

GREAT MOVERS

At last it was moving day.

Before anyone had even finished breakfast, six burly men began stomping through the house, taping boxes, lifting furniture, rolling up rugs, and making a lot of noise.

The movers arrived in a large green moving van with GREAT MOVERS written in large letters on the side. They all wore green shirts with GREAT MOVERS printed on the back.

"It could either mean they're great at moving furniture," Ollie said, "or it could mean they look fantastic on the dance floor."

Ava shot him a withering look.

"Watch out!" shouted Ma Peachey as two gigantic moving men bore down on them carrying a large chest of drawers. Ollie scooted out of the way just in time to avoid certain death.

"That was scary," Ollie said to no one in particular. "These are fast movers and frightening movers. But are they great movers? I think the jury is still out."

McTavish looked at Ollie, and Ollie looked back at McTavish.

"If only dogs could speak," said Ollie.

If dogs could speak, McTavish thought, *they'd tell humans to stop being so foolish.*

"Ho, ho, ho!" called Pa Peachey cheerily. "It's moving day! The birds are singing; the sky is blue; the sun is shining. I am so happy I could burst!"

"Oh, great," muttered Ava, imagining Pa Peachey bursting like an overfilled balloon and the family having to peel bits of him off the walls. Ava wished (not for the first time) that Pa Peachey would go back to his normal gloomy self. Moving was inconvenient, but having Pa Peachey act happy all the time was just plain disturbing.

Ma Peachey directed the action like a sheepdog trying to herd geese.

"This way!" she called loudly. And then a minute later, "No, not this way! That way!"

McTavish scurried this way and that to avoid the moving men, careful to prevent his

tail being stepped on or shut in a door. He didn't even have time to eat breakfast before someone had wrapped up his bowl in brown paper and packed it in a box.

Each box had a big label saying where it should go in the new house, but McTavish didn't need labels. He could tell just by sniffing.

Ava's boxes smelled like roses and earth and complicated ideas.

Ollie's boxes smelled like sneakers, idleness, and no girlfriends at all.

Betty's boxes smelled like books, woolly sweaters, and peppermint—with a most delicious hint of dog.

McTavish's own box contained his bed, his food, his toys, and his towel, and it smelled mainly like damp fur and meaty bones, which were two of the best smells in the world.

The moving men rolled up their sleeves. They wrapped and carried. They grunted and groaned. They stamped in and out of the house, time after time after time, until all the Peacheys' possessions were loaded onto the van.

Then they all stopped and sat down at the edge of the road to rest while Ma and Pa Peachey, Ava, Ollie, Betty, and McTavish spent a final few moments wandering through the house.

Now that it was empty, it didn't feel like home anymore.

All the rooms looked big and lonely. All the walls looked grubby, with outlines where pictures no longer hung and furniture no longer stood. Ollie ran from room to room shouting "Goodbye, goodbye!" because now that it was empty, the house had a very satisfying echo.

Betty looked at the empty house and remembered all the birthday parties she'd had—with presents and games and chocolate cake, because that was her favorite. She remembered all her first days of school— getting dressed in her bedroom, admiring her new clothes in the mirror, and feeling a little bit nervous and excited every year.

She remembered the first day McTavish had come home to live with them—how she had sewn his bed out of an old blanket stuffed with a sleeping bag, and how he had made himself right at home from that very first day.

She thought about Ma Peachey doing yoga and the weeks that Ollie, Ava, and she had learned to cook. She thought of happy games they'd played as a family and times she'd felt lonely and gone to sleep in Ma and Pa Peachey's bed.

Betty had taken her first step in this house. She had said her first word and sung her first song. She had learned to read in this house, played with her first friend, fought with Ava and Ollie, and made up again in this house. Nearly all the memories of her whole life had taken place here. And now she was leaving it behind.

Ava flung out her arms. "Metaphysics is a dark ocean without shores or lighthouse, strewn with many a philosophic wreck," she announced.

Everyone looked confused.

"Those are the words of Immanuel Kant," Ava said.

"Shame Immanuel Kant can't make any sense," Ollie said with a snicker.

"I shall never see these dear walls and floors and rooms and ceilings again," Betty whispered sadly.

In front of the house, the Great Movers all jumped aboard the van at once. Ollie had to admit that it was a pretty good move.

The Peacheys waved goodbye to the movers. Then they turned and waved goodbye to the house.

"Goodbye, house!" called Ollie.

"Goodbye, house!" called Ava.

"Goodbye, house," Ma Peachey said softly.

Pa Peachey just grinned, like a person who has won millions in the lottery.

"Thank you, house," whispered Betty. "You were the best house a person could ever want."

As they drove away, McTavish stuck his nose out the window, smelled all the smells of the old neighborhood for the last time, and woofed goodbye to his old life.

8

FEAR AND TREMBLING

It seemed impossible, but by the end of the day, all the boxes had been unloaded into the new house, all the sheets had been found, all the beds had been made, and most of the kitchen had been unpacked.

Ma Peachey made pancakes for supper (the Peacheys loved pancakes). They all went to bed a bit grubby because nobody could find soap or towels, but they were too tired to care.

Everyone woke up the next morning anxious to arrange all the things from the old house into the new house. They took books out of boxes and put them on shelves. They hung clothing up in closets and pinned posters to walls. Ava brought her own set of towels into her own bathroom and folded them neatly—knowing Ollie couldn't come in and throw them on the floor. She sorted all her philosophy books into alphabetical order so she could find any one quickly in an emergency.

Ollie arranged his bedroom so it looked like a man of the world lived there—with lots of pillows on his bed so it doubled as a couch, and posters of cool bands and race cars and exotic faraway places on the walls.

He stepped back at last and thought that all it was missing was a girlfriend.

Betty put everything in her new bedroom exactly where it had been in her old bedroom. The picture of a horse painted by an old French artist, the portrait of McTavish she'd drawn herself (which Ma Peachey had said was good enough to be framed), and the poster from her school's production of HMS *Pinafore* all went over her bed.

How interesting, Betty thought, that "home" seemed to be a picture that hung on the wall over your bed; rows of your favorite books on shelves; a pink, green, and yellow patchwork quilt that Ma Peachey had made; and sheets that smelled just right.

At the end of the second day, with all the books on shelves, all the pictures hung up, all the pots and pans in kitchen drawers, and all the clothes put away, the new house felt almost like home.

Betty felt a bit better with everything unpacked. If she squinted a little, she could almost pretend nothing had changed.

It wasn't that she didn't like the new house.

She liked her secret clubhouse. She liked the apple tree. She liked the fact that she could take McTavish to the park through a gate at the end of the yard.

She felt happy putting McTavish's water bowl in its proper place beside the fridge and hanging his leash on a hook by the front door. His bed could no longer fit under the stairs, but Betty had arranged it in a nice cozy corner with a good view of the family action.

All these things she liked.

What she didn't like was the fact that school started in less than a week and she would have no one to walk in with on the first day.

No one to sit next to.

No one to eat lunch with.

No one to giggle with in PE.

No one to help with her math homework.

No one to walk home with.

"Oh, don't you worry your head about such things, young Betty," Pa Peachey had said with the optimistic smile of a madman. "It will all turn out just fine."

How do you know it will all turn out just fine? Betty thought. Her father had turned into a happy freak, whistling and smiling every minute of the day, thinking only pleasant thoughts and not at all interested in reality.

"It's so creepy," Ollie said. "I wish someone would take him away and bring back the old Pa Peachey."

"All this good cheer is maddening," Ava said. "Especially first thing in the morning. It's like the real Pa Peachey has been abducted by aliens."

"We used to know where we were with the old Pa. Now anything could happen. He might break into song at any moment. Or start telling us how much he loves us." Ollie looked frightened.

Ava shook her head sadly and returned to reading *Fear and Trembling* by Søren Kierkegaard, a Danish philosopher.

"While we're on the subject of personality change," said Ma Peachey, "does anyone know where Betty has gone?"

"She's probably upstairs," said Ollie.

"Hmm," said Ma Peachey with a frown. "Has anyone seen McTavish?"

"Also probably upstairs," said Ollie.

"Hmm," said Ma Peachey with another frown.

Ma Peachey entered Betty's bedroom, got down on her hands and knees, and crawled to the back of Betty's closet. She knocked on the secret door.

"May I come in?" she asked.

"Yes," said Betty.

"Woof," said McTavish.

Ma Peachey crawled in. It was very crowded in the tiny space.

"Hello," said Ma Peachey. "I hope I'm not interrupting."

"You're not," said Betty.

"Betty," said Ma Peachey. "Are you worried about your new school?"

Betty looked at Ma Peachey. McTavish looked at her, too.

"I thought so," said Ma Peachey.

Betty said nothing.

Ma Peachey kissed Betty's hair. "I think you'll find that it is terribly difficult the first day, a little bit difficult the second day, but by the third day it will hardly feel difficult at all."

"How do you know?" asked Betty.

"Well . . . I just do," said Ma Peachey.

"What if you're wrong?" asked Betty. "What if it's terrible the first day, unspeakable the second day, and worse than anything that's ever happened in all of human history on the third day?"

"I would be immensely surprised if that turned out to be the case," said Ma Peachey.

"But it's possible," said Betty.

Ma Peachey sighed. "I guess we will just have to wait and see."

9

NEW SCHOOL

Betty zipped up her new plaid skirt. She buttoned her new white blouse. She pulled her new sweater over her head. She brushed her hair, she washed her face, and she headed downstairs for breakfast.

"Well, Betty," Pa Peachey said in his cheerful voice. "We're both new kids today. I don't know about you, but I certainly am nervous! What if no one talks to me at lunch?

What if everyone forgets my name? Ho, ho, ho, that would certainly ruin my day!"

"Your name will be engraved on your office door," Betty said. "No one will forget it."

"Ha, ha! Good point," Pa Peachey said. "Well, I'd better be going. Doesn't do to be late on your first day now, does it? Good luck, Betty. Cheerio! Pip-pip! Ta-ta!"

Ma Peachey sighed and kissed her husband goodbye. She'd married a pessimist and now found herself living with Mr. Happy-All-the-Time. It was confusing, to say the least.

"Come along, Betty," Ma Peachey said gently. "Have some toast, and then McTavish and I will walk you to school."

Ollie and Ava didn't start school for another week, so they were still in bed. But they both leaned out their bedroom windows to wave goodbye. "Good luck!" they called.

McTavish wagged his tail.

The neighborhood was filled with children on their way to school. Out the corner of one eye, Betty looked at each child they passed. They all seemed too old or too young to be in her class, and everyone seemed to be walking with a friend or a group of friends. Occasionally someone stopped to admire McTavish, but nobody stopped to admire Betty.

At last they arrived at the new school.

"It will get better," Ma Peachey said as she kissed Betty goodbye. "Trust me."

Betty knelt to kiss McTavish goodbye, but for once he didn't stare into her eyes with sympathy or offer his paw. In fact, McTavish didn't seem at all interested in Betty. Ears pricked, nose in the air, legs stiff, eyes focused on the middle distance, McTavish suddenly lunged forward with the force and speed of a race car.

"McTavish!" cried Ma Peachey. "Come back!"

"McTavish!" called Betty. "Come back!"

"McTavish, stop!"

"McTavish, sit!"

"McTavish, heel!"

But McTavish was off. If he could hear Betty and Ma Peachey calling, he gave no sign.

"Come back!" Betty shouted again. And then she began to run. She couldn't see what McTavish was chasing, but she had to stop him.

"Come back, Betty!" cried Ma Peachey, and she set off running as well.

"Stop!" Betty and Ma Peachey both shouted. "Stop that dog!"

All the children who'd gathered outside the school gates for the first day of school saw a furry golden streak fly past. Nobody could see what it was chasing.

"Stop that dog!" shouted one mother.

"Stop that dog!" shouted a teacher.

"Stop the doggie!" shouted a group of girls.

"Grab him!" shouted some boys.

"Tell him to sit!" shouted a father.

"Stop him!"

"Grab him!"

"Get him!"

"Hold him!"

And then with one voice, the parents, the children, the teachers, Betty, and Ma Peachey all shouted, "STOP THAT DOG!"

But McTavish didn't stop. He kept on

running until the whole school was running after him and everybody was shouting "STOP!"

They ran up one side of the playground and down the other. They ran clockwise around the school, chasing McTavish, then they turned and ran back the other way. They ran in through the front door and out through the back door. They ran up the stairs and down the stairs. They ran through the parking lot and all around the basketball courts.

"Stop running this instant, or you'll have a week of detention!" shouted Mr. Moriarty, the assistant principal.

"Stop running this instant, or you'll have no dessert for a month!" shouted Miss Peckish, the lunch lady.

"Stop running this instant, or you will not appear in the holiday play!" shouted Miss Ibsen, the drama teacher.

"Stop running this instant, or you'll be expelled from school forever!" shouted Miss Stern, the principal. She seemed to be yelling

this at McTavish, forgetting that McTavish didn't go to school in the first place.

McTavish did not stop.

In fact, he seemed to be running faster than ever.

10

GOTCHA!

The entrance to Betty's new school was scattered with book bags. Children leaned panting against walls or sprawled flat out on the ground.

A few of the more athletic students were still chasing McTavish, who seemed to have slowed slightly. At one point, he looked over his shoulder to see how many people were still running after him.

The moment that McTavish looked over his shoulder was the exact moment that Mr. Scrubbins, the school custodian, jumped out from behind the bike shed and grabbed him around the middle.

"GOTCHA!" Mr. Scrubbins cried.

McTavish was caught fair and square. He didn't even struggle, possibly because he was feeling quite winded.

Everybody cheered.

"Mr. Scrubbins caught McTavish! Mr. Scrubbins caught McTavish! Mr. Scrubbins is a hero!"

Ma Peachey approached Mr. Scrubbins.

"I am so terribly sorry," she said. "I cannot tell you how ashamed I am of our dear McTavish. He is normally the best-behaved dog in the world, but today he seems to have lost all control." She gave McTavish a severe look.

Mr. Scrubbins chuckled. "There's no harm done," he said. "Everybody's had a good run, and no one minds a bit of excitement on the first day of school. Do we, kids?"

"No!" shouted all the kids.

"Of course they've missed their first assembly, but I bet no one minds that either."

"No!" shouted all the kids.

"I don't think anyone will ever forget this particular first day of school," said Miss Stern, the principal. And although she did her very best to live up to her name, she did smile a little.

Ma Peachey was relieved that no one was angry.

Well, she thought, *this has been a most*

exciting morning, but it's time to take McTavish home.

"Come along, McTavish," Ma Peachey said.

But where was McTavish now?

She saw a large group of children standing in a circle. At the center of the circle was Betty. And in Betty's arms was McTavish.

Stepping closer, Ma Peachey could hear bits of conversation.

"I wish I had a dog like McTavish."

"He is so adorable."

"Could I come to your house after school and play?"

"You're so lucky. Your dog is amazing."

"Can I pat him?"

"How old is he?"

"What breed is he?"

"Can I hold him?"

"If I came over to your house, could we take him to the park?"

In the middle of the circle, Betty was answering questions. When McTavish suddenly turned and swiped her face with his tongue, everybody laughed, including Betty.

A girl standing right behind Betty leaned over and said in a quiet voice, "Will you sit with me in class?"

Betty turned to look.

"Jasmin!" she cried. "Are you in my class?"

Jasmin nodded.

"I think it's time for everyone to report to classrooms," said the not-very-stern Miss Stern.

"And I think it's time for McTavish to go home," said Ma Peachey. She knelt to hug Betty and whisper in her ear. "Is it OK if we leave now?" she asked.

Betty nodded.

"Of course we'll be right here to pick you up after school," Ma Peachey said.

"With McTavish?" chimed all the children at once.

"With McTavish," said Ma Peachey.

"See you later, McTavish," Betty said, and kissed his furry head.

"See you later, McTavish," said Jasmin.

"See you later, McTavish!" shouted all the children together.

See you later, thought McTavish, with a satisfied wag of his tail.

11

THE MOST WELL-BEHAVED DOG IN THE WORLD

"Come along, McTavish," Ma Peachey said. "What a morning you've had! Running around like a wild thing, getting the whole school to chase you."

McTavish glanced up at her with an innocent expression.

Ma Peachey smiled. "I don't know how you do it, but you always seem to make things better."

McTavish trotted alongside Ma Peachey

like the most well-behaved dog in the world.

They walked along for a little while in silence. Ma Peachey was running over the events of the morning in her head.

One thing bothered her.

"McTavish," Ma Peachey said, "what on earth were you chasing? I never did see what it was."

It is worth remembering that one of the great advantages of being a dog is that you don't have to answer awkward questions. In fact, being a dog makes answering questions optional pretty much all the time.

So it wasn't really a problem that McTavish decided not to answer Ma Peachey's question.

All that day, Ma Peachey worked in her new office at the top of the house. When it was time to pick Betty up from school, Ma Peachey put McTavish on his leash and headed back down the road. When they arrived, the children all gathered around McTavish as if he were a celebrity.

Betty came out of the school door arm in arm with Jasmin.

"How was your first day?" Ma Peachey asked. But she already knew the answer.

That night at dinner, Betty couldn't stop smiling.

Pa Peachey, however, did not whistle. He did not sing. He did not smile. He did not chuckle. He did not once say, "Always look on the bright side," or "Isn't it grand just to be alive?"

Instead, he muttered moodily, "A job is basically just a lot of work."

Ava and Ollie looked at each other.

Then he grumbled, "A job is just years of miserable toil from cradle to grave with the occasional day off for good behavior."

Betty and Ma Peachey exchanged glances.

"In fact," Pa Peachey said, "you could say there is nothing in life so miserable as a job."

From his basket in the corner, McTavish raised his head and pricked his ears.

"Even a new job," Pa Peachey added, "which is pretty much the same as any other job. Only more so."

Ava grinned.

Ollie punched the air.

Ma Peachey leaned over and kissed her husband on the cheek.

Betty got up from her chair and hugged him.

This was the Pa Peachey they knew.

This was the grumpy, miserable, crabby, bad-tempered Pa Peachey the family knew and loved.

"Welcome back, Pa!" they chorused at once, but Pa Peachey just frowned.

Then Betty told Ava and Ollie the story of chasing McTavish around and around the school, and how it led to her making lots of new friends.

"But what was McTavish chasing?" Ava asked. "A cat? A burglar? A cat burglar?"

"Yes, what was McTavish chasing?" Ollie asked. "A zombie? A ghost? A monster?"

Everybody looked at McTavish, who was dozing happily in his comfy bed.

"McTavish?" Ma Peachey asked, fixing him with the sort of direct gaze that nearly always worked on Ollie, Ava, and Betty.

But McTavish merely opened one eye halfway, looked back at Ma Peachey with an expression of total innocence, and then closed it again.

"Well," said Ma Peachey, "I suppose we may never find out what McTavish was chasing."

And then she smiled to herself, wondering if McTavish had actually been chasing anything at all.